SUPERTATO

VEGGIES IN THE VALLEY OF DOOM

Brilliant librarians and fabulous teachers
TO THE RESCUE!

SIMON & SCHUSTER
First published in Great Britain in 2018
by Simon & Schuster UK Ltd
1st Floor, 222 Gray's Inn Road, London, WC1X 8HB
A CBS Company

A CIP catalogue record for this book is available
from the British Library upon request

978-1-4711-7630-2 (HB)
978-1-4711-7170-3 (PB)
978-1-4711-7171-0 (eBook)

Printed in Italy

1 3 5 7 9 10 8 6 4 2

SUPERTATO
VEGGIES IN THE VALLEY OF DOOM

by Sue Hendra and Paul Linnet

SIMON & SCHUSTER

London New York Sydney Toronto New Delhi

It was night-time in the supermarket and the veggies were complaining. "There's nothing to do!" whined Pineapple.

"We could play hide-and-seek?" said Broccoli.
"I'm GREAT at hide-and-seek!"

"What a splendid idea," said Supertato.

So the veggies ran off to hide
and Supertato started to count.

"One . . . two . . . three . . .

. . . four hundred and ninety-eight . . .
four hundred and ninety-nine . . . five hundred!

Ready or not,
here I come!"

"Hmmm, they must be around here somewhere," thought Supertato.

I think I've found
you, Carrot."

"You've found ME,"
said Carrot, "but look
what I'VE found . . .

. . . it's a treasure map!"

"You might be right," said Supertato, "and it seems to be leading to the gardening aisle."

As the veggies gathered round, SOMEONE was watching.

"Ooooo, treasure," thought The Evil Pea, from his hiding place.

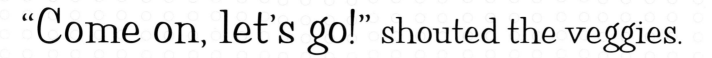

"Come on, let's go!" shouted the veggies.

"Not so fast," said Supertato. "First we're going to need some supplies."

And he rounded up some water, biscuits, rope and, of course, a pair of oven gloves.

Eh?

But the entrance to the gardening aisle was a wall of plants.

"We'll never get through that!" said Carrot.

"Ah," said Supertato, "that's what the water's for . . . " and with that, he poured it into the pots.

Slurp, **slurp**, **slurp** went the plants and up they sprang, clearing the way ahead.

"Thanks, Supertato, we were gasping!"
"Wow," said Tomato. "I didn't know plants could talk!"

"Come on everyone, this way," said Carrot. "The map says we need to go through the Valley of Doom."

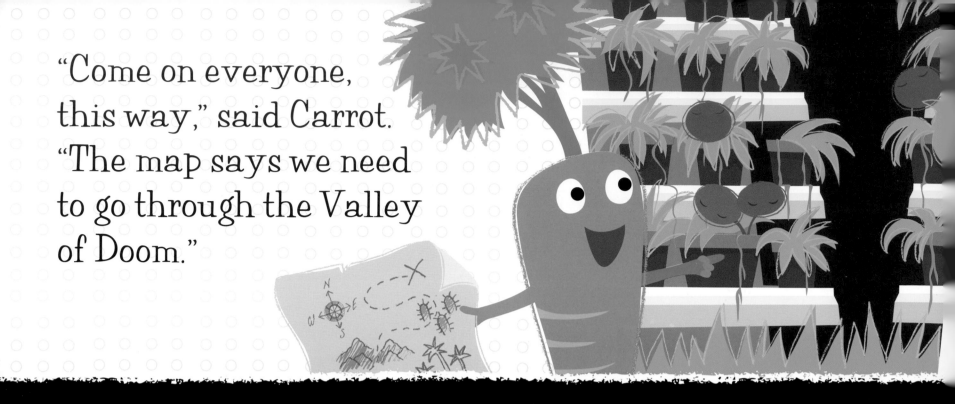

"Hmmm . . . why is it called the Valley of Doom?" wondered Pineapple . . .

. . . but he didn't wonder for long.

"Quick, Pineapple, it's crunch time," shouted Supertato. "Throw me the biscuits!"

Luckily, the biscuits did the trick and Supertato and the veggies were soon out of danger. PHEW!

But now they'd reached a dead end.
"This must be Cactus Canyon," said Carrot.

"We'll get prickled to pieces!" cried Tomato.
"How will we ever get through?"

"With oven gloves, of course!" said Supertato,
and soon they were back on their way.

It was a long trek through the desert.
"I can't go on," said Tomato.
"Yes, you can," said Supertato.
"Together we're all going to make it."

After hours of walking they were finally
out of the desert.

"I can see a treasure chest!" shouted Carrot.
"We're almost there!"

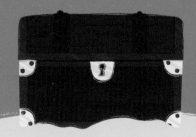

But Supertato and the veggies
were so excited, they didn't see . . .

. . . the quicksand!

"Help! Help!" they yelled. "We're sinking fast!"

"*Mwah ha ha ha ha!*" shrieked The Evil Pea.
"You ARE in a sticky situation!"

"Oh dear," said one cactus to another,
"is this the end for Supertato and the veggies?"

Maybe it was. With Supertato
in the quicksand, who could help
these veggies in distress?

"Well, don't look at me!"
shouted the pea.
"The treasure's mine, ALL mine!"

"Please, please help us, Pea," called the veggies.
"Before it's too late . . ."

"OH, ALL RIGHT," snapped the pea.
"IF I MUST."

Supertato threw the rope and the pea pulled them to safety.

"You saved us!" squealed the veggies.

"You're a hero!"

"No, I'm not, I'm evil! All that 'Help! Help! Help!' was giving me a headache, that's all!"

Supertato smiled. The moment had come. Everyone crowded around the treasure chest – it was time to see what was inside . . .

"SURPRISE!!!!!" yelled Broccoli, popping out of the treasure chest. "I told you I was GREAT at hide-and-seek!"

Supertato and the gang started
the long walk home.

"I didn't have you down as one of
the good guys, Pea," said Supertato,
"but maybe I was wrong . . ."

"*Mwah ha ha ha ha!* Whatever you say, Supertato," sniggered the pea.